THE WACKY ~~AL~~ ANIMAL ALPHABET

BY AMY KOZE

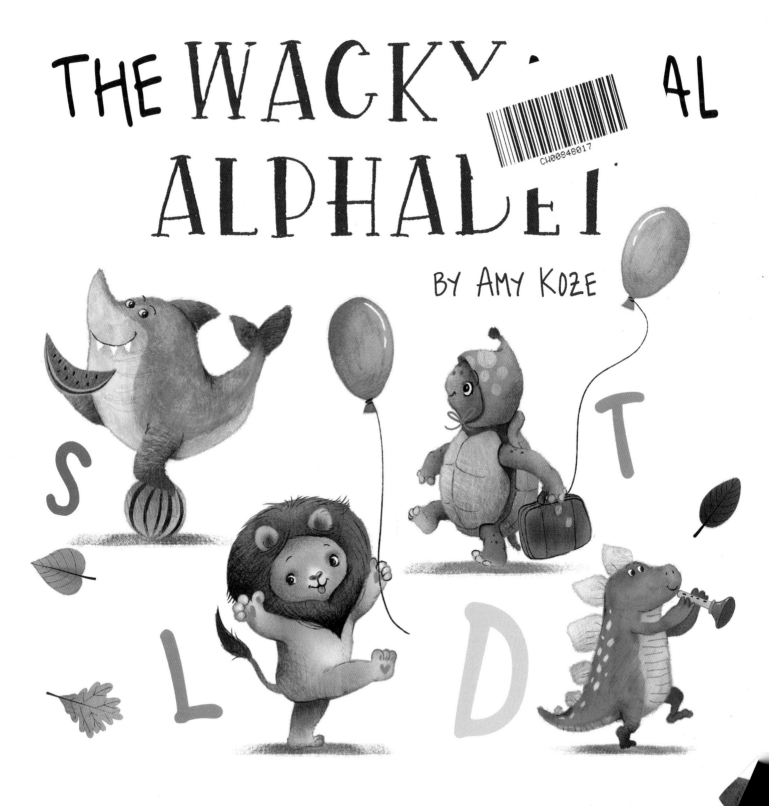

Have you ever heard about the **curious** alphabet forest?

Where live
creatures,
without doubt,
very odd,
maybe even
the oddest!

They can do very **unusual things...** They are the strangest animals **you will ever see!**

Have you ever seen a **cat that sings,** a juggling giraffe, or a lion that **likes candy?**

Turn the page to find out who they are!

The anteater
with a spinning top.

Aa

Be careful! Don't get
dizzy and drop!

The brown **bear** riding a motorbike.

Bb

Oh! What an unusual sight!

The furry cat
who just loves to sing.

Cc

Bath time is the best
for some jazz and swing!

The **dinosaur**
who plays the flute.

Dd

Such jolly tunes! Isn't he cute?

The **elephant**
who can fly a plane.

Ee

Whoosh and off he goes again!

The **flamingo**
who takes photos

Ff

wherever she goes!

The giraffe
who can juggle acorns

Gg

since the day she was born!

The **hedgehog**

who keeps asking when

Hh

Christmas day will come again!

The **iguana**
whose wildest dream

Ii

is to eat chocolate ice cream!

The jellyfish
who found a rubber duck!

J j

She must have been in luck!

The **kangaroo**
who filled her pockets

Kk

with tasty veggies
from the market!

The joyful **Lion**
who bought a lollipop

Ll

and some fairy floss
from the candy shop!

The little **mouse**
whose graceful ballet

Mm

simply blew the crowd away!

The **nutria**
who is proud to own

Nn

some very cool new headphones!

The **octopus**
wearing red goggles

Oo

who likes to give
cuddles and tickles!

The adventurous **penguin**
going on a trip,

Pp

sailing off on his
home-made pirate ship!

The **quail**
who plays guitar

Qq

and hopes to be a popstar!

The **raccoon**
who loves berries

Rr

of all sorts and varieties!

The acrobatic shark
with a watermelon slice.

Ss

He can balance on a
watermelon on ice!

The **turtle**
going on holiday

Tt

so he can have fun
and play all day!

The **unicorn**
so sweet and cuddly,

Uu

her pillow is her best buddy!

The **vulture**
heading to the market

Vv

in a fancy space rocket!

The **wolf**
who finds riding a bike

W w

super fun and easy as pie!

The **x-ray fish**
brushing his teeth

Xx

after eating a very sweet treat!

The excited yak
eager to see his new ball

Yy

bounce off the wall!

The little **zebra**
holding a  huge balloon,

Zz

wishing he could fly to the moon!

CAN YOU REMEMBER THE WACKY ANIMALS' NAMES?

"The adventure of life is to learn"

- William Arthur Ward

For my precious little ones, Kiara & Kayden,
who help me realise that life is an adventure,
with so many things to learn and discover - E.K.O

Printed in Great Britain
by Amazon

79941327R10020